This book belongs to:

____

____

ABOUT YOU:

I love doing ...

I hate doing ...

My favourite ninja ...

My favourite movie ...

My favourite song ...

My favourite book ...

I would describe myself in these three words:

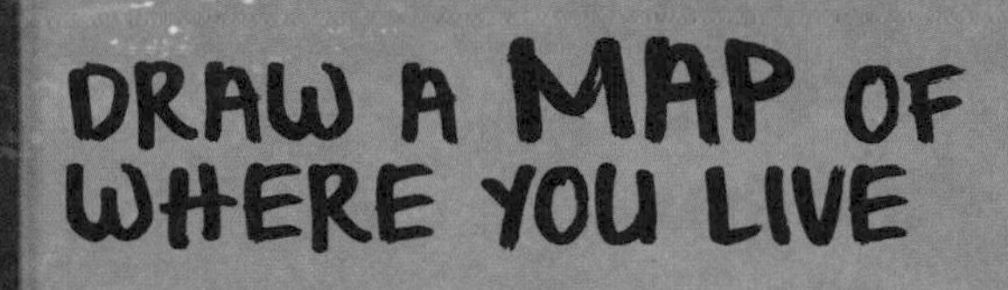
DRAW A MAP OF
WHERE YOU LIVE

A DAY IN THE LIFE OF THE NINJA TEAM

6:00 A.M. WAKEY-WAKEY!

6:30 A.M. BREAKFAST (SHOWER FIRST! NO SLEEPWALKING NINJA ALLOWED AT THE BREAKFAST TABLE.)

7:00 A.M. TRAINING

10:00 A.M. MORNING SNACK

10:30 A.M. MORE TRAINING

1:00 P.M. LUNCH (TRAINING INCREASES APPETITE!)

2:00 P.M. SOME MORE TRAINING

5:00 P.M. HOMEWORK

6:00 P.M. FREE TIME (VIDEO GAMES!)

7:00 P.M. DINNER (PREFERABLY PIZZA)

AFTER 8 P.M. FREE TIME (MORE VIDEO GAMES - FOR THOSE WHO HAVEN'T ALREADY FALLEN ASLEEP)

WHAT IS **YOUR** DAILY DRILL?

1.

2.

3.

4.

5.

6.

7.

8.

9.

10.

YOU OWN A RESTAURANT FOR NINJA!

What's on the menu?

there is nothing on the menu you get what you Dizerve

Breakfast:

Karma

Lunch: Karma

Dinner: Karma

Snacks/Treats: Karma

Don't forget to
include drinks!

THINGS A NINJA SHOULD KNOW

What else do you think a **ninja** needs to know?

IN THE SPOTLIGHT

Imagine you're a famous **ninja**.

What would you say to your fans?

What would you be famous for?

What's your plan?

BE LIKE MASTER WU

If you became Master Wu for a day...

What would you do?

Who would you train?

What would you teach them?

Where would you visit?

What would you eat?

YOU'VE FOUND PIRATE TREASURE! AARGH!

What would you do first?

1. Run away from the pirates.

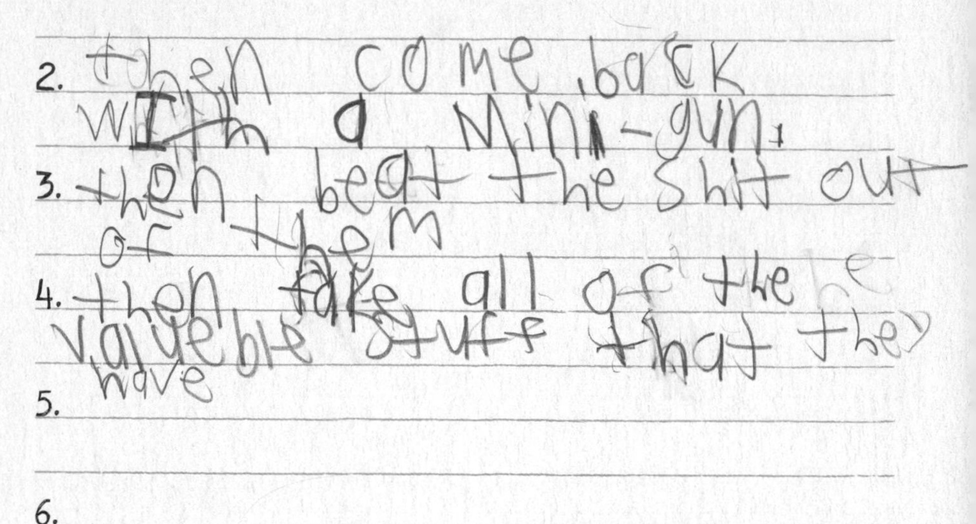

then come back
with a mini-gun.
then beat the shit out
of them
then take all of the
valuebie stuff that they
have

2.

3.

4.

5.

6.

7.

8.

MY WORST DAY EVER

Write about the craziest day you've ever had.

What would have made your day totally awesome instead?

YOU'VE FOUND A DJINN IN A MAGIC LAMP!

What are your three wishes?

WISH ONE:

WISH TWO:

WISH THREE:

Watch out! With your third wish, the Djinn could trap you in the lamp!

MAKE THE NINJA UNRECOGNIZABLE!

Now design your own wanted poster

DISGUSTING PIZZA!

Imagine the grossest pizza possible!

What would be on it?

INGREDIENTS:

WHAT WOULD YOUR PIZZA BE CALLED?

DESIGN YOUR OWN FLAG

It can even be a pirate flag!

NICE!

You suddenly age by
60 years!

How do you **feel**? What do you **look** like?
What do you do for **fun**?

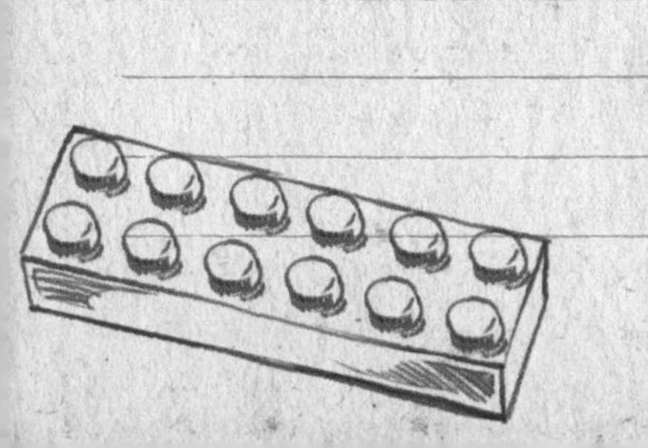

WRITE YOUR OWN COMIC
ADD TITLE
THE SKY PIRATES HAVE BEEN PREYING ON SEASIDE TOWNS IN THEIR RAID ZEPPELIN.
ZANE IS CLOSING IN, BUT ...

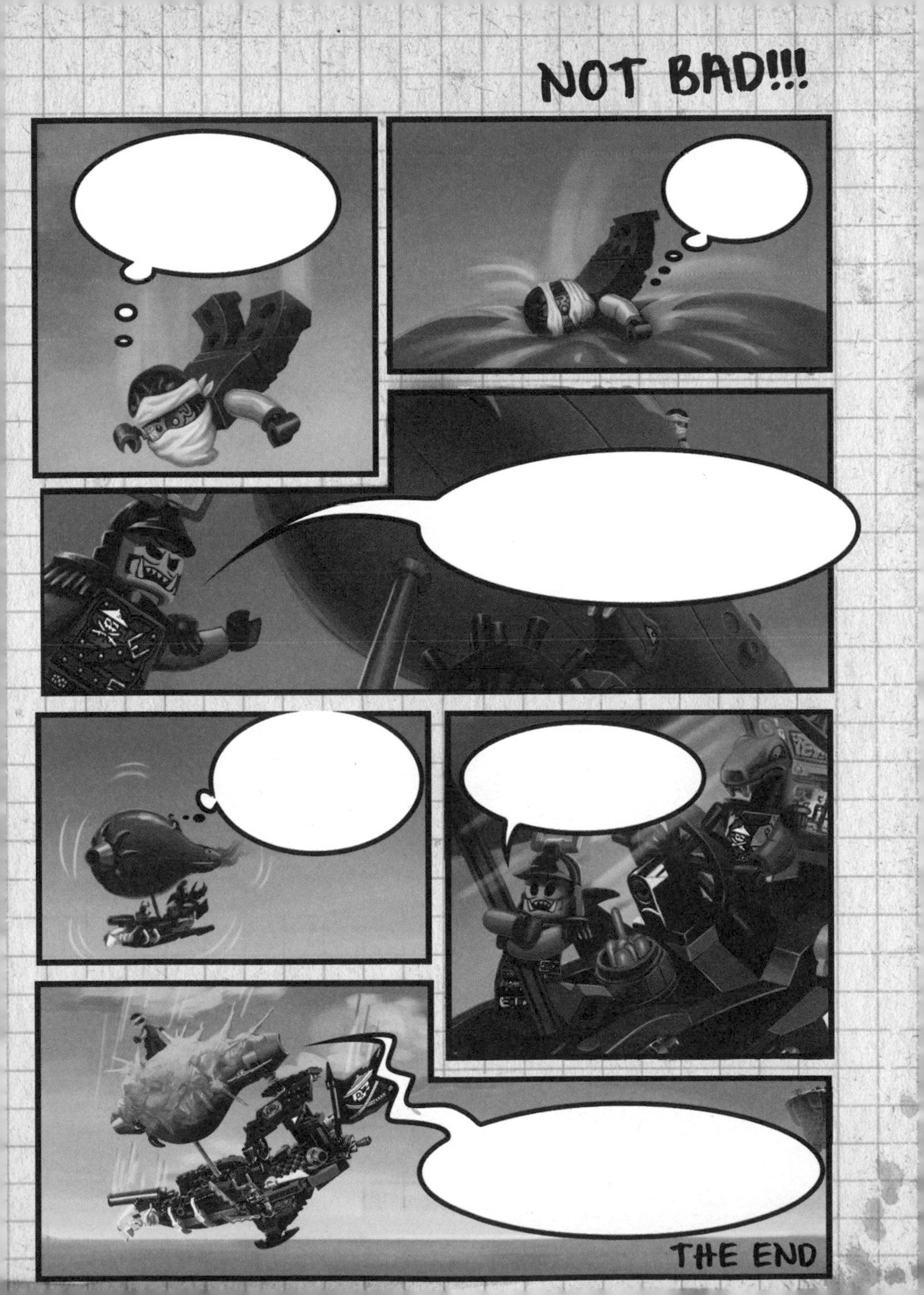
NOT BAD!!!
THE END

NINJA ALWAYS LOOK COOL!

Design a cool **ninja outfit** that you'd like to wear.

There's nothing like a good team!

Draw your dream ninja team and describe their awesome powers.

WHAT IS THE BEST ADVENTURE YOU'VE EVER HAD?

HOW WOULD YOU SURVIVE IN THE WILD?

Here's what Jay would take with him:

1. The book *How to Survive in the Wild.*

2. A TV. (How can you live without it?)

3. A sofa.

4. The whole house, just in case the sofa gets damaged in the open air.

5. A few best friends.

6. Two big sacks of snacks and a store full of video games.

7. A training dojo, of course!

What would you take with you?

1.

2.

3.

4.

5.

6.

Who likes building more than

CLEANING?

List ten of your favourite things to build with LEGO® bricks:

1.

2.

3.

4.

5.

6.

7.

8.

9.

10.

FRIENDS AND FAMILY
HALL OF FAME

Draw your friends and family members as ninja.

WHO IS THIS?

FRIENDS AND FAMILY

HALL OF FAME

PETS INCLUDED!

HA HA :)
FUNNY!

IMAGINE YOU ARE A NINJA WITH THE POWER TO TIME TRAVEL:

You would travel to ...

You would meet ...

You would wear ...

WHAT WOULD YOU DO IF YOU HAD THE TIME BLADES?

Forward:

Slow-Mo:

Pause:

Reversal:

Finish the story, young ninja. Perhaps it will be passed from ninja to ninja for many years to come.

The night was so dark that the ninja could barely see his own hands. He'd already bumped into a tree twice and fallen into a puddle, but he still moved on. He had to finish his mission. To his relief he saw a small light ahead. It was Master Wu showing him the way. At last the ninja knew which direction to go in. Suddenly he heard a loud rustle along the path and a dark figure jumped out of the bushes ...

THE TALE OF THE DARK SHADOW

The story continues:

DRAW WHAT YOU LIKE BEST
ABOUT YOUR HOME TOWN

BEWARE OF GHOOOOSTS!

Draw a ghost that would **scare** even Master Wu!

EEK!

IT'S YOUR BIRTHDAY!

Design the party decorations and a ninja-themed birthday cake.

HAPPY BIRTHDAY!

A SIP OF SOME
WONDROUS
TEA ...

If you had your own tea shop, where would you get new flavours? What skills would you like your tea to enhance?

For example, extract of dried carrot, nettle leaves and juicy jelly beans could help your observation skills.

The tea I make with rose petals and oak bark gives me strength, energy and keeps my mind fresh.

WHAT SHOULD A REAL NINJA BE LIKE?

You've got thirty seconds to come up with eight great comparisons!

Fast as a ... cheetah

Brave as a ...

Dangerous as a ...

Skillful as a ...

Flexible as a ...

Quiet as a ...

Cunning as a ...

Supple as a ...

Sharp as a ...

YOU ARE MAKING A NINJA MOVIE!

Describe what your action-adventure film is about and give it two possible endings.

HAPPY ENDING ...

CLIFFHANGER ENDING ...

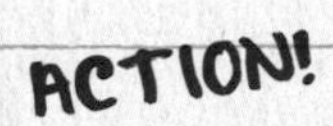

Design a supercool

NINJA MOTORCYCLE

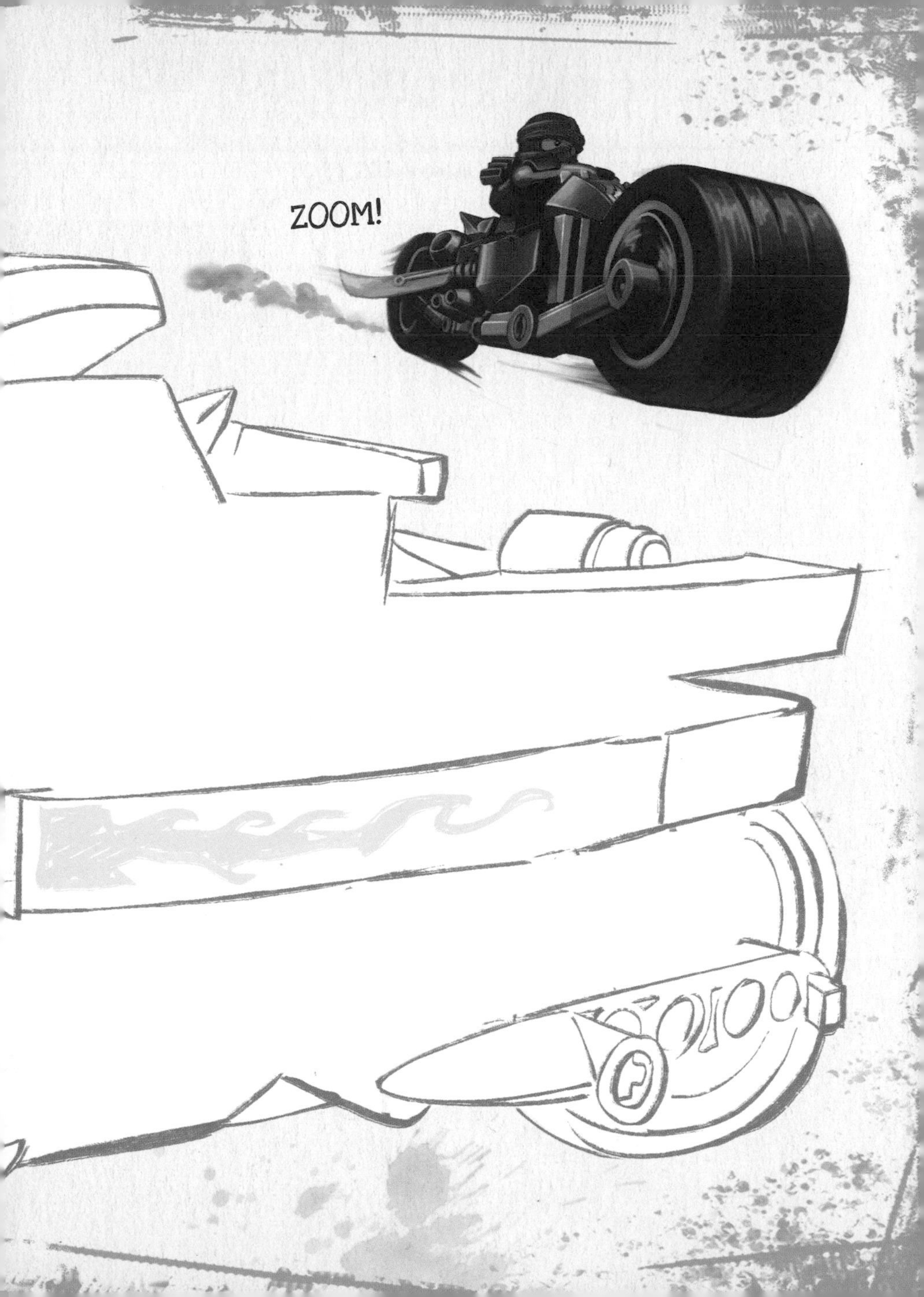
ZOOM!

FINISH THIS SPOOKY COMIC

Continue Kai's story here, or make up a new story.

POSTCARD FROM NINJAGO CITY

You're visiting Ninjago's realms.
Write a postcard to a friend.

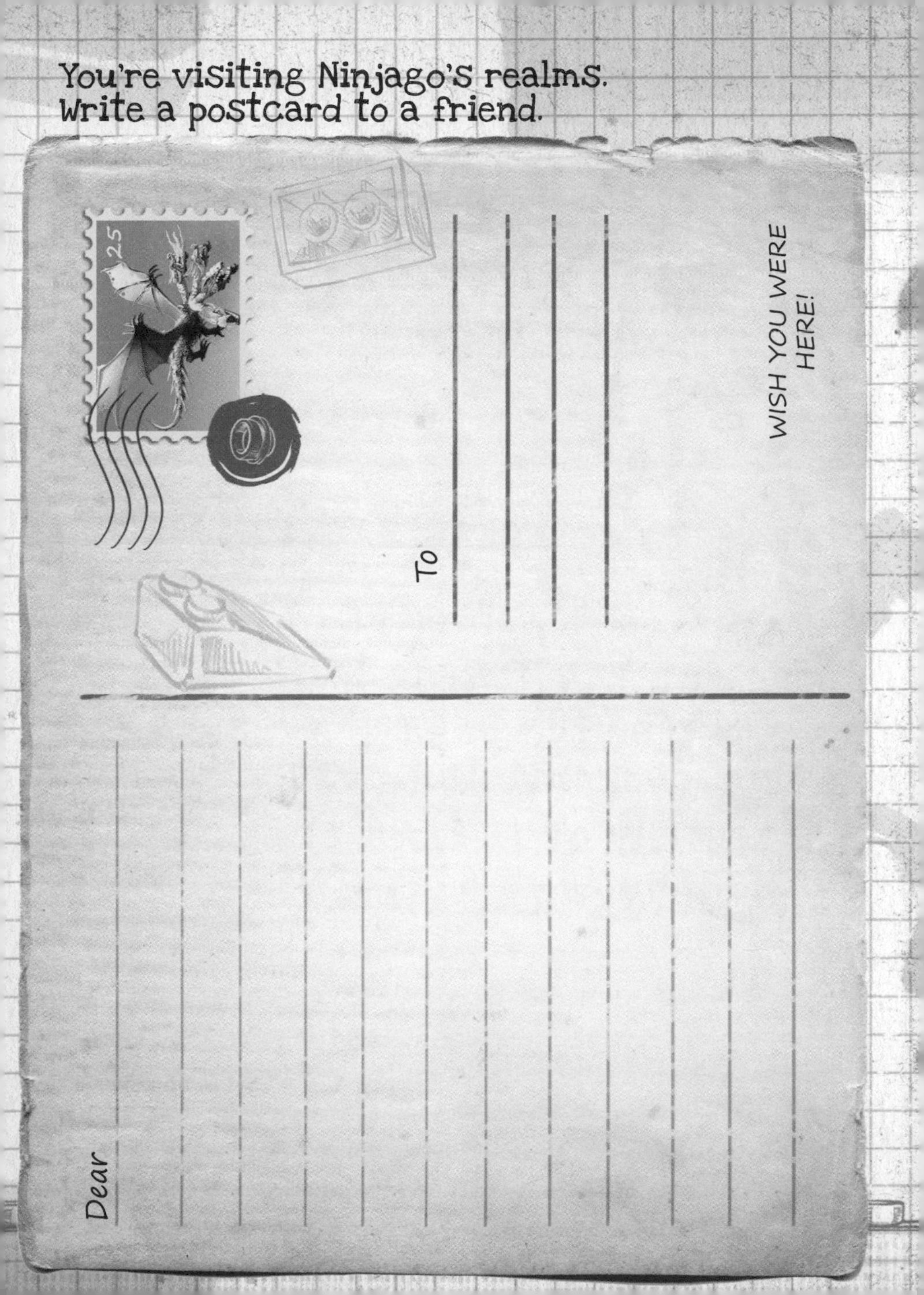

CAN YOU READ BACKWARDS?

???

A GNOL, GNOL EMIT OGA
EHT TSRIF RETSAM FO
UZTIJNIPS DEGROF RUOF
SNOPAEW DNA DESU
MEHT OT ETAERC EHT
DLROW FO OGAJNIN.

Now write your own secret message:

Now, can you write it backwards?

CREATE YOUR OWN
NINJA CODE OF LAWS

I would never:

I will always guard:

I promise:

I would do anything to:

I will always be ready to:

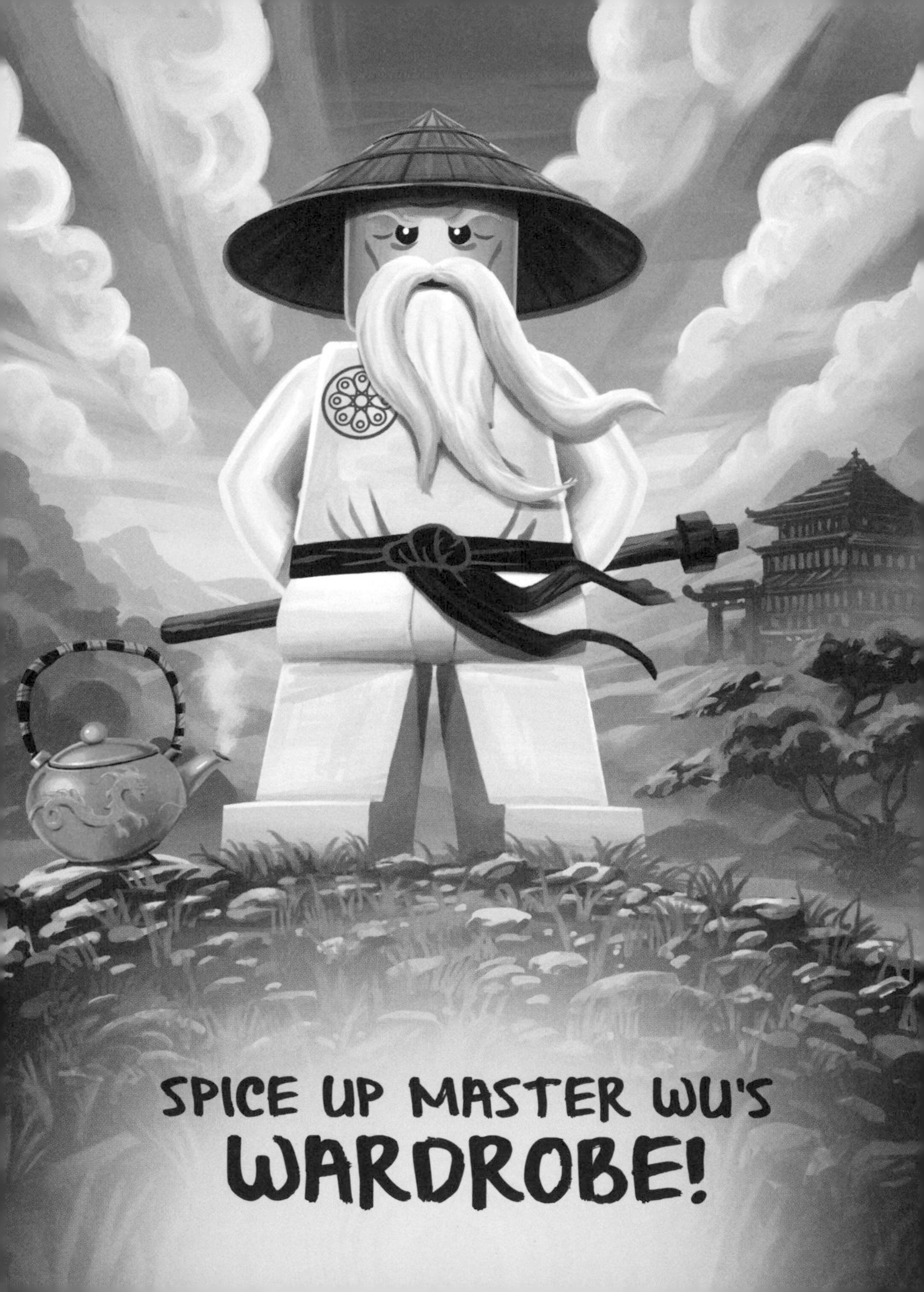

SPICE UP MASTER WU'S WARDROBE!

Design new outfits for him.

TAKE PART IN
THE SPINJITZU
TOURNAMENT!!!
FILL IN THE
APPLICATION
FORM!

NINJA TOURNAMENT APPLICATION FORM

Your ninja nickname:

The element you control:

Your ninja colour:

Your weapon of choice:

Name of a Spinjitzu move you've created?

Height: Weight:

How many hours do you sleep for?

What healthy foods do you eat?

What special skills do you have?

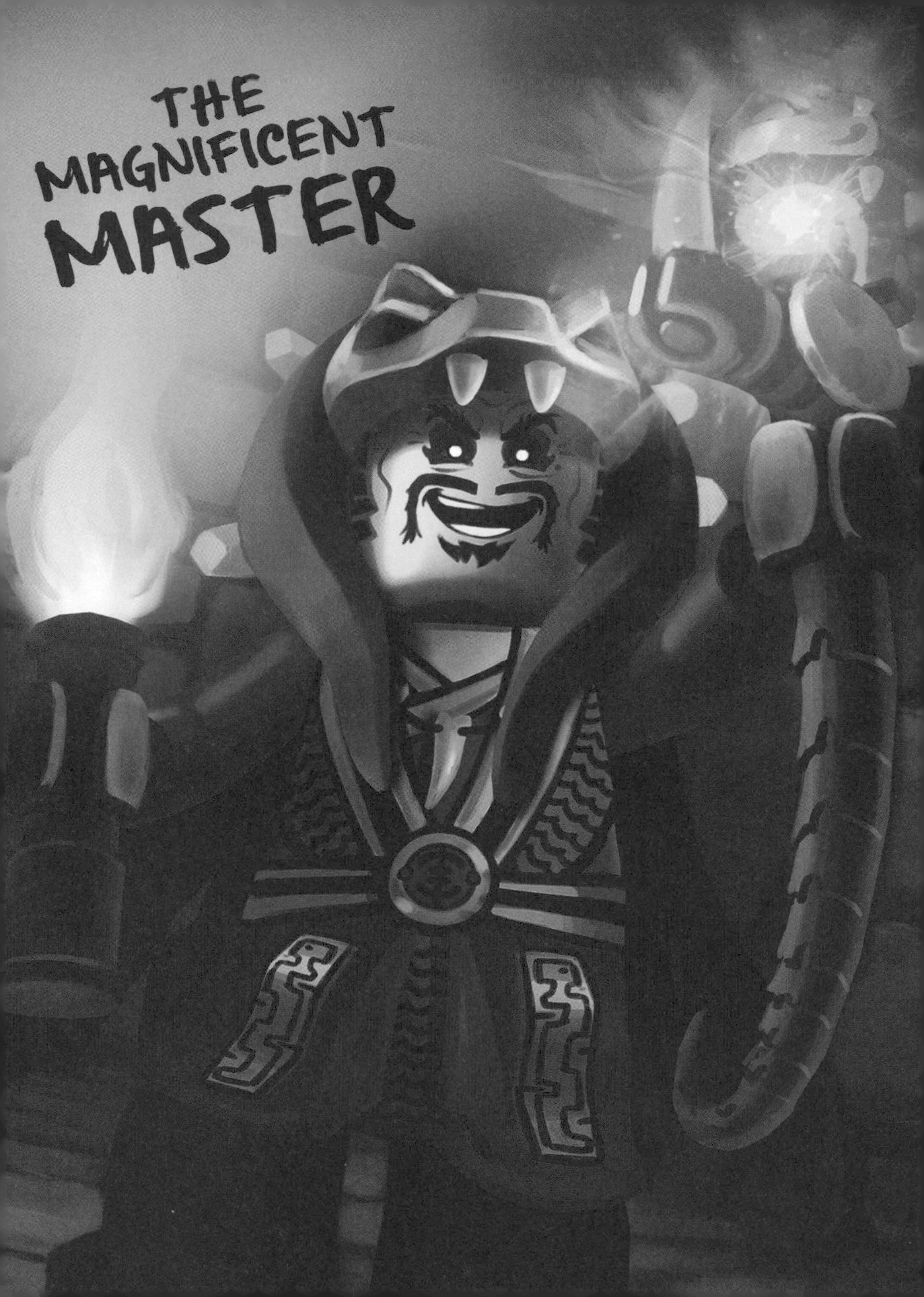
THE MAGNIFICENT MASTER

Draw yourself as **an Elemental Master** in action.

WHAT A HUGE HOUSE! WHY NOT MAKE IT NINJA HEADQUARTERS?

Draw the things the ninja would need in each room.

WHAT ARE YOUR FAVOURITE NINJA **JOKES** AND SAYINGS?

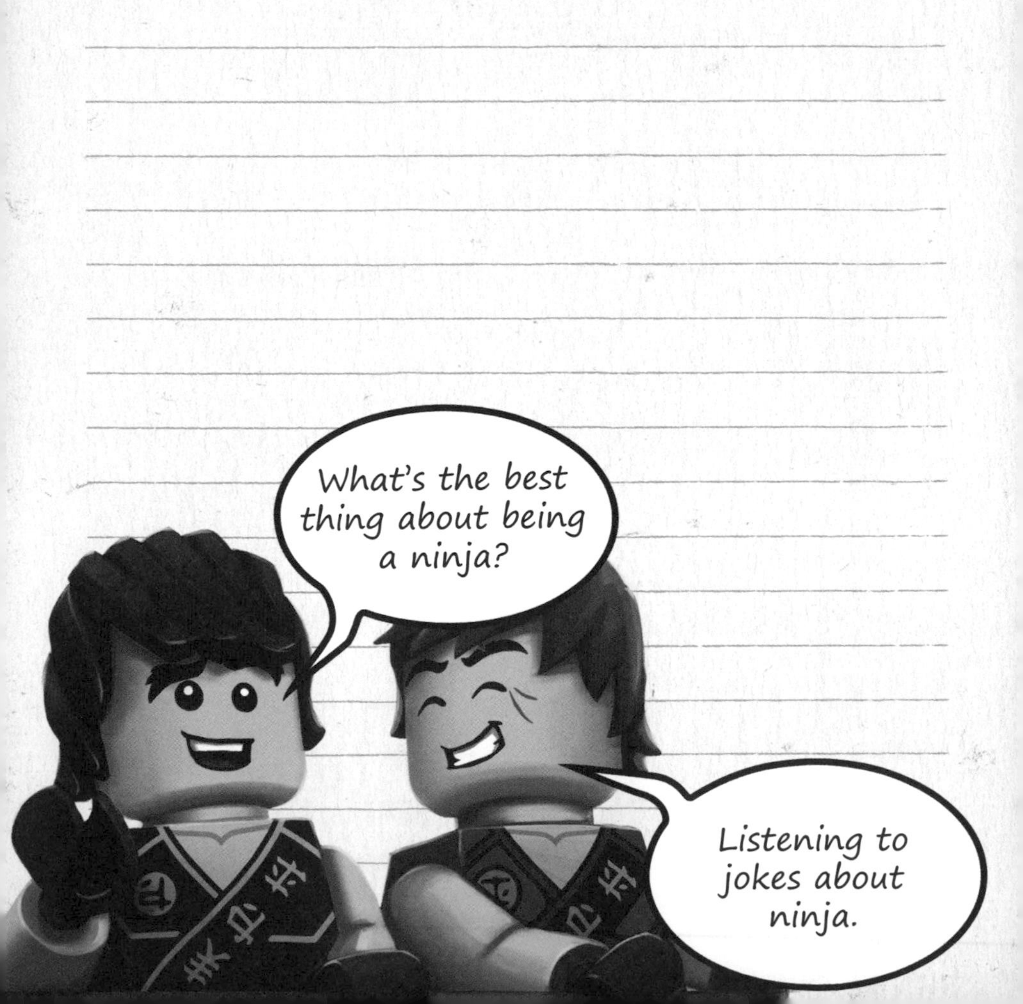

Ha ha ha!!!

DESIGN YOUR OWN TRAINING DUMMY

7½

What would it look like after training?

A TRUE NINJA IS A MASTER OF CAMOUFLAGE!

Can you spot 5 ninja hidden in this picture?

A ninja has disguised themselves on this page.
Draw who it is.

it is master wu

A ninja can hide even on an empty page.

DESIGN YOUR OWN

SUPER WEAPON!

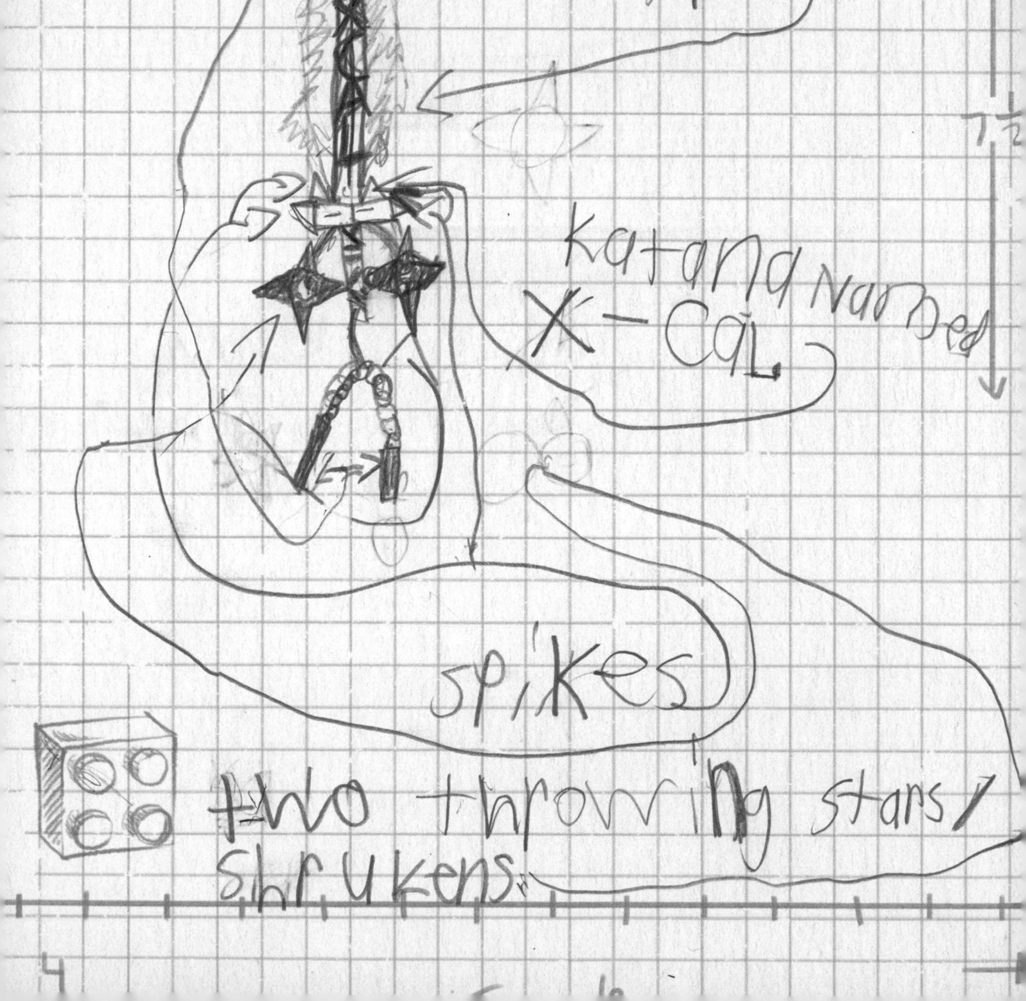

$17\frac{1}{2}$

MAKE YOUR OWN
GRAFFITI

WHAT A WORK
OF GENIUS

NINJA'S SECRETS

Real ninja never give away their secrets.

Especially when
the secret is
really important!

But you can use a special ninja code to write them down.

We will teach you how to do it!

Want to know what code to use? Turn the page to find out!

Write a list of your deepest secrets

In each word swap the first letter with the last one. KOMEWORH SI GNTERESTINI OT EM.

... or replace the letters with numbers:
A-1, B-2, C-3, D-4, etc.

CHOOSE YOUR TRAINING OPTION:

PATH OF A DRAGON:

- flap your arms as if you want to take off
- swing your leg in all directions as if it was a dragon's tail
- practise a menacing dragon expression in the mirror

SAMURAI'S WALK:

- clean your room without complaining
- develop your own samurai's cry
- practise samurai's walk to crazy, loud music

NINDROID'S UPGRADE:

- do laps around your computer
- read a book backwards
- play your favourite computer game blindfolded

CREATE YOUR OWN TRAINING PLAN:

WRITE TEN THINGS YOU WOULD DO IF YOU WERE A YOUNG NINJA!

1. I would look for other ninja in the neighbourhood.

2. I would form a super awesome team.

3.

4.

5.

6.

7.

8.

9.

10.

THINGS I DO WHEN I AM AN ANGRY NINJA!

IMAGINE HOW YOU'D ACT IF YOU WERE AN ANGRY NINJA.

If I was angry
I would lose ...

I would shout ...

To cool off
I would go ...

I would play ...

WHAT WOULD THE NINJA'S GREATEST ENEMY LOOK LIKE?

DRAW THEM HERE.

Ha! That's really scary, it ALMOST gives me goosebumps.

THE NINJA KNOW HOW POWERFUL A DRAGON IS.

What would your dragon look like?

Draw and describe it.

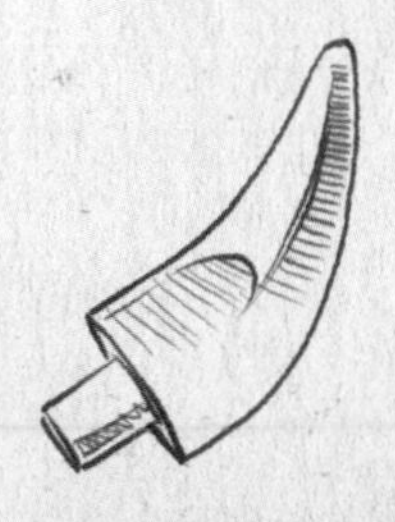

NINJA NIGHTMARE!

WHAT IS THE STRANGEST DREAM OR

NIGHTMARE

YOU'VE EVER HAD?

ALL NINJA HAVE THEIR OWN SIGNATURES!
JAY
Lloyd
Nya
Kai
Cole

Have you got your own?

NOW ASK YOUR FRIENDS
TO WRITE THEIR

AUTOGRAPHS

HERE!

THE NINJA LOVE TO PLAY GAMES.

List some of your favourite games below.

sas4 zombie
assult sas 3 zombie
ass ult sas 2

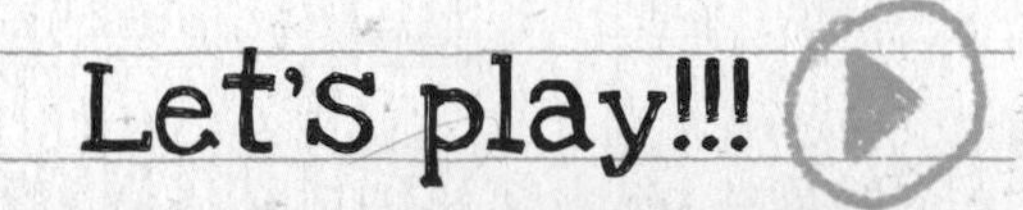

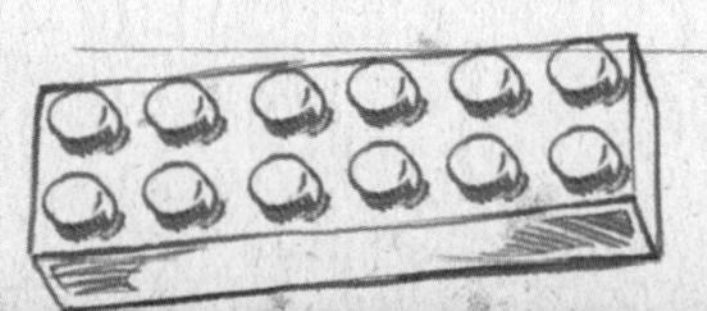

NINJA SIGNS

EACH NINJA HAS THEIR OWN SIGN.

Draw a sign that represents you.

HYPNOSIS

Don't stare at this spiral for too long!

How can the ninja defend themselves from hypnosis?

Turning a mirror on the enemy is a good idea. What other ideas can you think of?

Master Wu loves his AIRSHIP!

Draw what your ninja team's air fortress looks like.

WITH THIS MECH, YOU CAN BE INVINCIBLE!!!

What would your mech look like?
Draw it below and then write what it can do.

Try to build it with LEGO bricks too!

NINJA TRAIN TO
PERFECTION
EVERY DAY ...

... ALMOST

What are you particularly good at?

What else would you like to be good at?

NOTEBOOK

Use these pages to draw the ninja or whatever you want. :)

NOTEBOOK

NOTEBOOK

NOTEBOOK

NOTEBOOK

NOTEBOOK

NOTEBOOK

NOTEBOOK

NOTEBOOK

WHICH SPINJITZU MASTER WOULD YOU MOST LIKE TO BE?

Kai: Nothing is impossible for you! You love action and know no fear. Your energy and vigour give others the will to fight. You're a vital part of the team!

Nya: You get along with everyone and can find a solution to every problem. You like to keep busy, and the team can always count on you to get them out of trouble.

Zane: You spend a lot of time thinking and analysing situations. You have a cool-headed approach and don't let your emotions get the better of you. You see more than others, which makes you a great member of every ninja team.